Dear Parent:

Congratulations! Your child is taking the first steps on an exciting journey. The destination? Independent reading!

STEP INTO READING® will help your child get there. The program offers five steps to reading success. Each step includes fun stories and colorful art. There are also Step into Reading Sticker Books, Step into Reading Math Readers, Step into Reading Write-In Readers, Step into Reading Phonics Readers, and Step into Reading Phonics First Steps! Boxed Sets—a complete literacy program with something for every child.

Learning to Read, Step by Step!

Ready to Read   Preschool–Kindergarten
• big type and easy words • rhyme and rhythm • picture clues
For children who know the alphabet and are eager to begin reading.

Reading with Help   Preschool–Grade 1
• basic vocabulary • short sentences • simple stories
For children who recognize familiar words and sound out new words with help.

Reading on Your Own   Grades 1–3
• engaging characters • easy-to-follow plots • popular topics
For children who are ready to read on their own.

Reading Paragraphs   Grades 2–3
• challenging vocabulary • short paragraphs • exciting stories
For newly independent readers who read simple sentences with confidence.

Ready for Chapters   Grades 2–4
• chapters • longer paragraphs • full-color art
For children who want to take the plunge into chapter books but still like colorful pictures.

STEP INTO READING® is designed to give every child a successful reading experience. The grade levels are only guides. Children can progress through the steps at their own speed, developing confidence in their reading, no matter what their grade. Remember, a lifetime love of reading starts with a single step!

Thomas the Tank Engine & Friends™

CREATED BY BRITT ALLCROFT

Based on The Railway Series by The Reverend W Awdry.

© 2009 Gullane (Thomas) LLC.

HIT entertainment

Visit us on the Web!
www.stepintoreading.com
www.thomasandfriends.com

Educators and librarians, for a variety of teaching tools, visit us at
www.randomhouse.com/teachers

Library of Congress Cataloging-in-Publication Data
Thomas and the jet engine / based on The railway series by the Reverend W. Awdry ; illustrated by Richard Courtney. — 1st ed.
   p. cm. — (Step into reading. Step 1)
"Thomas the Tank Engine & Friends"
"Created by Britt Allcroft"
"Based on The Railway Series by The Reverend W Awdry"
Summary: When the jet engine that Thomas the Tank Engine is transporting to the airport accidentally gets switched on, Thomas suddenly becomes the fastest engine on the island.
ISBN 978-0-375-84289-4 (trade pbk.) — ISBN 978-0-375-95626-3 (lib. bdg.)
[1. Railroad trains—Fiction. 2. Speed—Fiction. 3. Jet propulsion—Fiction.]
I. Courtney, Richard, ill. II. Awdry, W.
PZ7.T36945944 2009 [E]—dc22 2008009228

Printed in the United States of America
10 9 8 7 6 5   First Edition

THOMAS & FRIENDS

Thomas and the Jet Engine

Based on *The Railway Series*
by The Reverend W Awdry

Illustrated by Richard Courtney

Random House 🏠 New York

Thomas likes
to go fast.
Gordon thinks
he is faster.

Thomas must take
a jet engine
to the airport.

A jet engine goes
by pushing hot air
out its back.

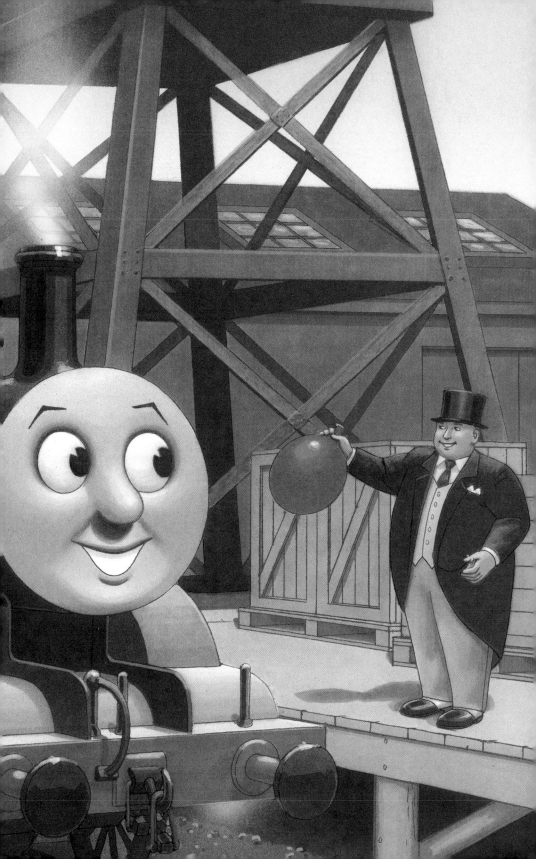

It is like a balloon
full of air.

When you let it go,
off it zooms.

Cranky does not look.
His hook bumps
the switch.

Click!

The jet engine
starts up!
Vroom! Vroom!

14

The jet engine rockets

Thomas up the track.

Zoom! Zoom!

Clear the lines!

Runaway train!

Thomas passes Percy.
Whoosh!

Thomas passes Henry.

Whoosh!

Hi, Gordon!

Vroom!

Bye, Gordon!

Zoom!

At last,
the jet engine runs
out of fuel.
Phew!

Thomas chuffs
to the airport
on his own steam!

Peep! Peep!

Back at the Shed,
Gordon ignores Thomas.
Humph!

Gordon may not be
a jet engine . . .

. . . but he *is*
full of hot air!